WITHDRAWN

ESCAPE FROM PLANET ALCATRAZ

VOYAGE TO THE METAL MOON

BY MICHAEL DAHL

ILLUSTRATED BY PATRICIO CLAREY

STONE ARCH BOOKS
a capstone imprint

Escape from Planet Alcatraz is published by
Stone Arch Books
A Capstone Imprint
1710 Roe Crest Drive
North Mankato, Minnesota 56003
www.capstonepub.com

Library of Congress Cataloging-in-Publication Data
Names: Dahl, Michael, author. | Clarey, Patricio, 1978– illustrator.
Title: Voyage to the metal moon / by Michael Dahl ; illustrated by
   Patricio Clarey.
Description: North Mankato, MN : Stone Arch Books, a Capstone
   imprint, [2020] | Series: Escape from planet Alcatraz
Identifiers: LCCN 2019005619 (print) | LCCN 2019007671 (ebook) |
   ISBN 9781496583215 (eBook PDF) | ISBN 9781496583147
   (library binding)
Subjects: LCSH: Science fiction. | Prisons—Juvenile fiction. |
   Stowaways—Juvenile fiction. | Escapes—Juvenile fiction. |
   Extraterrestrial beings—Juvenile fiction. | Extrasolar planets—
   Juvenile fiction. | Adventure stories. | CYAC: Science fiction. |
   Prisons—Fiction. | Stowaways—Fiction. | Escapes—Fiction. |
   Extraterrestrial beings—Fiction. | Extrasolar planets—Fiction. |
   Adventure and adventurers—Fiction. | LCGFT: Science fiction. |
   Action and adventure fiction.
Classification: LCC PZ7.D15134 (ebook) | LCC PZ7.D15134 Vr 2020
   (print) | DDC 813.54 [Fic]—dc23
LC record available at https://lccn.loc.gov/2019005619

Summary: Zak Nine and his alien friend, Erro, are trying to escape the
prison planet known as Alcatraz. Their latest plan involves hiding on
another spaceship and riding it to freedom. Unfortunately for the boys,
the ship lands on Alcatraz's nearby metallic moon, a prison just as
deadly as Alcatraz itself!

Editor: Aaron J. Sautter
Designer: Kay Fraser
Production Specialist: Katy LaVigne

Design elements: Shutterstock: Agustina Camilion, A-Star, Dima Zel,
Draw, Wing, Zep, Hybrid, Graphics, Metallic Citizen

TABLE OF CONTENTS

ERRO

PLATEAU OF LENG

PHANTOM FOREST

POISON SEA

VULCAN MOUNTAINS

LAKE OF GOLD

METAL MOON

DIAMOND MINES

MONSTER ZOO

PITS of NO RETURN

PRISON STRONGHOLDS

SWAMP of FLAME

SCARLET JUNGLE

PRISON ENERGY DRIVES

SPACE PORT PRISONER INTAKE

ABYSS of GIANTS

ZAK

THE PRISONERS

ZAK NINE

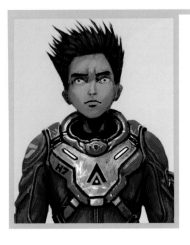

Zak is a teenage boy from Earth Base Zeta. He dreams of piloting a star fighter one day. Zak is very brave and is a quick thinker. But his enthusiasm often leads him into trouble.

ERRO

Erro is a teenage furling from the planet Quom. He has the fur, long tail, sharp eyes, and claws of his species. Erro is often impatient with Zak's reckless ways. But he shares his friend's love of adventure.

THE PRISON PLANET

Alcatraz . . . there is no escape from this terrifying prison planet. It's filled with dungeons, traps, endless deserts, and other dangers. Zak Nine and his alien friend, Erro, are trapped here. They had sneaked onto a ship hoping to see an awesome space battle. But the ship landed on Alcatraz instead. Now they have to work together if they ever hope to escape!

ERRO'S STORY . . . A RISKY PLAN >>>

Right now Zak and I are hiding in an Alcatraz spaceport hangar. He talked me into hiding inside a prison ship to escape. Zak thinks that when the ship lands on another planet, we can get away and find a way home. It's a risky plan, but I trust my human friend. . . .

>>>>

CHAPTER ONE:
STOWAWAYS

Zak and I are hanging from the underside of a prison transport ship. We are close to an open cargo door.

My claws are gripping the ship's energy cables. It is dark inside the hangar, and the guards cannot see us.

This is all Zak's idea. For a human boy with no tail, he certainly likes to climb and hang from things.

"Just a little farther," Zak whispers.

I flex my tail and then leap upward. I jump from the energy cable to the cargo door.

When I get inside the door, I lean down toward Zak. He grabs my paw. I pull him up, and we are both inside the ship.

"Finally," I say. "It took us two hours to get up here."

"We had to be careful, didn't we?" asks Zak. "We don't want the guards to see us."

He is right. The Alcatraz guards are everywhere.

ZZZZHHHHP!

The cargo door slides shut. We barely made it in time.

"That was close! They're getting ready to take off," Zak says.

In the dark cargo area, we find extra flight suits hanging on the wall.

The suits are bulky. They are big enough to fit the huge guards. We each hide inside one.

Soon, the roar of the ship's engines rings in my ears.

Why did I let Zak talk me into this?

CHAPTER TWO:
TO THE MOON

We are not sure where this ship is heading.

"Anywhere it goes has to be better than Alcatraz," Zak had told me.

Maybe we will land on a planet where we can contact our families.

ZZZZRRRRRRR!!

Suddenly the ship's engines
sound different.

"I think we are slowing down,"
I tell Zak.

"Oh no . . . we can't be landing already!" says Zak.

Zak steps over to a porthole.

"We're just above Alcatraz," he says. "We're not moving."

I join my friend next to the round window. We have docked next to a large, shiny sphere. It floats high above the prison planet.

It is a moon made of metal.

CHAPTER THREE:
PRISON SATELLITE

Prisoners in flight suits are moving on the metal surface. Heavy magnetic boots keep them attached to the metal. They are working on tall cylinders.

We are not in space. The moon appears to fly high above the planet. The cylinders must be part of the moon's engines.

WHUMMP! WHUMMP!

There are footsteps above us. Through the porthole we see many people marching off of the ship.

Alcatraz guards lead lines of prisoners off the ship. They are all in chains.

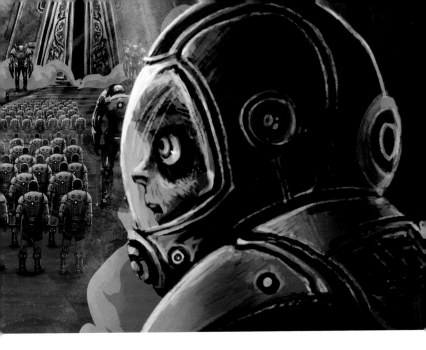

The guards force the prisoners
toward a large door that leads inside
the metal moon.

"This is just another prison," I say.
"A prison the size of a moon."

"This stinks!" says Zak. "Now we have to stay in here and go back to Alcatraz."

"When do you think the ship will return—" I start to ask.

WHUMMP! WHUMMP!

Oh no! The guards are back!

"Down in the cargo hold!" we hear one of them snarl. "I think I saw something moving at the porthole when I was outside."

"We cannot stay here," I say.

Zak grabs a pair of magnetic boots and tosses them to me. "Here! Take these!" he yells. Then he grabs another pair for himself.

We quickly remove our flight suits and slip the boots onto our feet. My fur is caught in the straps.

"Come on, Erro!" Zak says and pulls me toward the cargo door. He pulls at the edge, and the door swings open.

Just then, a guard holding a laser spear enters the room. We jump through the cargo door and begin to fall.

CHAPTER FOUR:
UPSIDE-DOWN CHASE

The strong magnetic boots swing me in a wide circle. I land feetfirst on the moon with a loud clang.

"AAAAGGGHHH!" Zak is screaming.

Is he in pain? I wonder. But then I see him pointing and shouting in amazement.

We both stare at the massive shape
of Alcatraz hanging high above us.

ZZZZHOOOOM!

A laser beam suddenly explodes next to us! Armed guards pour out of the transport ship.

Zak and I run across the moon's curved surface.

"We cannot go back to the ship,"
I say. "There is no way to escape."

Zak looks up at the prison planet
hanging overhead.

"I know a way," he says with a smile.

CHAPTER FIVE:
FREE FALL

Five guards with jet packs quickly
zoom toward us. We cannot outrun them.

Zak bends down and looks at my feet.
"Your boots," he whispers to me.

"What about them?" I ask.

He reaches over and turns off my
magnetic boots. Then he turns his off too.

I start to fall away from the metal moon. Gravity is pulling me back to Alcatraz.

Now it is my turn to scream!

Without thinking, I grab onto Zak with my tail.

"You are going to kill us!" I shout at him.

But I am shouting in my own language. He does not understand me.

One guard zooms in close to us. He is so close that I can see the drool on his tusks.

"What took you so long?"
Zak shouts at the guard. Then he
grabs the guard's leg.

The guard screams. With our
extra weight, we are dragging the
guard with us. Now we are all falling
toward Alcatraz.

However, the guard's jet pack is still
working. As we fall toward the planet,
the jet rockets help us slow down.

Below us, a bright-red jungle grows
closer and closer.

When we are a few feet above the
trees, Zak lets go of the guard's leg.

"Thanks for the ride!" Zak shouts.

The guard's jet pack slingshots him back into the sky. He is carried far beyond the jungle.

To stop our fall, I grab Zak's hand and wrap my tail around a thick red branch.

I can barely stop panting. But we have escaped.

The thick jungle will help us hide. Hopefully we will find another way to escape the prison planet. . . .

GLOSSARY

cylinder (SIL-uhn-dur)—a shape with flat, circular ends and sides shaped like a tube

dungeon (DUHN-juhn)—a prison, usually underground

flight suit (FLITE soot)—a one-piece suit that protects a pilot

hangar (HANG-ur)—a large building in which aircraft are kept

laser (LAY-zur)—a thin, intense beam of light

magnetic (mag-NET-ik)—having the properties of a magnet

porthole (PORT-hohl)—a small, round window in the side of a ship

slingshot (SLING-shot)—to suddenly move forward or upward very quickly

species (SPEE-sheez)—a group of living things that share similar features

sphere (SFIHR)—a round, solid shape like a basketball or globe

stowaway (STOH-uh-way)—someone who hides in a plane, ship, or other vehicle to travel without being seen

TALK ABOUT IT

1. Erro and Zak tried to hide on a prison ship to escape Alcatraz. Do you think this was a good plan? If not, what would you have done differently? Explain your answer.

2. How do you think Zak and Erro felt when the ship stopped at the metal moon? How would you feel if your escape plan had failed so quickly?

3. Zak and Erro jump out of the cargo door when the guards find them. What other ways do you think they could have avoided being caught?

WRITE ABOUT IT

1. Zak and Erro are amazed when they see planet Alcatraz in the sky above them. Write about a time when you saw something that looked strange from a different angle. Describe what seemed strange about it.

2. Zak and Erro returned to planet Alcatraz by holding on to the guard with the jet pack. Write a new ending to the story using your own ideas for how the boys could have escaped from the prison guards.

ABOUT THE AUTHOR

Michael Dahl is the author of more than 300 books for young readers, including the bestselling Library of Doom series. He is a huge fan of Star Trek, Star Wars, and Doctor Who. He has a fear of closed-in spaces, but has visited several prisons, dungeons, and strongholds, both ancient and modern. He made a daring escape from each one. Luckily, the guards still haven't found him.

ABOUT THE ILLUSTRATOR

Patricio Clarey was born in 1978 in Argentina. He graduated in fine arts at the School of Visual Arts Martín Malharro, specializing in illustration and graphic design. Patricio currently lives in Barcelona, Spain, where he works as a freelance graphic designer and illustrator. He has created several comics and graphic novels, and his work has been featured in several books and other publications. Patricio is working on launching his first art book, *Attractor*.